To the ongoing presence of Theodor S. Geisel . . . Dr. Seuss.
Thanks, Herb.
—Audrey Geisel

Published in the United States by Random House Children's Books,
a division of Penguin Random House LLC, New York.
This edition with revised text and new illustrations
was originally published by Random House Children's Books in 1994.

Random House and the colophon are registered trademarks
of Penguin Random House LLC.

Visit us on the Web!
Seussville.com
randomhousekids.com

Educators and librarians, for a variety of teaching tools, visit us at
RHTeachersLibrarians.com

Library of Congress Cataloging-in-Publication Data
Name: Seuss, Dr.
Title: Daisy-head Mayzie / by Dr. Seuss.
Description: First edition. | New York : Random House, 2016. |
"Originally published by Random House Children's Books, in 1994." |
Summary: Young Mayzie McGrew becomes a sensation when a daisy grows
out of the top of her head, and everyone attempts to get rid of it.
Identifiers: LCCN 2015019699 | ISBN 978-0-553-53900-4 (trade) |
ISBN 978-0-553-53906-6 (lib. bdg.)
Subjects: | CYAC: Stories in rhyme. | Daisies—Fiction. | Fame—Fiction. |
Humorous stories.
Classification: LCC PZ8.3.S477 Dai 2016 | DDC [E]—dc23

Printed in the United States of America   10 9 8 7 6 5 4 3 2 1

Daisy-Head Mayzie

By Dr. Seuss

with illustrations based on sketches by the author

Random House New York

It's hard to believe such a thing could be true,
And I hope such a thing never happens to you.
But it happened, they say, to poor Mayzie McGrew.

It happened like this. She was sitting one day,
At her desk, in her school, in her usual way,
When she felt a small *twitch* on the top of her head.
So Mayzie looked up. And she almost dropped dead.
Something peculiar was going on there . . .

A daisy was sprouting right out of her hair!

BOING!

Behind her was sitting young Herman (Butch) Stroodel.
"This looks like a daisy up here on her noodle!
It doesn't make sense! Why it *couldn't* be so!
A noodle's no place for a daisy to grow!"
Then up spoke another boy, Einstein Van Tass,
The brightest young boy in the whole of the class,
"It's a very odd place to be sprouting a daisy.
But, nevertheless, one IS growing on Mayzie!"

"Hey! Lookit," cried Butch, "right here in this room!
Daisy-Head Mayzie! She's bursting in bloom!"

Miss Sneetcher, the teacher, came rushing up quick.
"Such nonsense! Some child is playing a trick!
Which one of you boys stuck that thing in her hair?
You *know* that a daisy could never grow there!"
"But, Teacher," said Butch, "I saw the thing rise
Right out of her head with my very own eyes.
Just give it a yank if you think I tell lies!"

Miss Sneetcher had heard quite enough of this talk.
"Mayzie! Hold still! Let me get at that stalk!"

"OUCH!" hollered Mayzie.

"Quit yanking," Butch said. "You're giving her pains.
I'll bet that those roots go way down in her brains!"

The kids in the room started shouting like crazy:
"Daisy-Head! Daisy-Head! DAISY-HEAD MAYZIE!"

"Children! Be quiet!"

Miss Sneetcher was puzzled. "Good grief and alas!
To think this has happened right here in my class!
I've taught in this room twenty years. Maybe more.
But I've never seen anything like this before!
I'll have to report it. You'll just have to come
To the Principal's office and show Mr. Grumm!"

Now the Principal, good Mr. Gregory Grumm,

Was a very wise man, just as smart as they come.

He knew more than anyone else in this nation

About long division and multiplication.

He knew all the answers. Why oceans are deep,

Why skies are so high, and why mountains are steep.

He should have the answer to this thing on Mayzie. . . .

"My word!" he declared. "It's a genuine daisy!

I've seen them quite often in fields growing wild.

But never before on the head of a child.

Now what in the world ever made this thing sprout?

I have no idea. *But I'm going to find out!*

"It says here . . . it says, daisies grow on the land.
They grow between rocks. They grow also in sand.
It mentions, right here, they can grow in a pot.
But mention the head of a girl, it does not!

"Daisies, it says, sometimes grow in Alaska.

Also Missouri, Rhode Island, Nebraska.

They grow in Japan and in Spain and Peru,

In India, France, and in Idaho, too.

They grow in South Boston. And also in Rome.

But WHY should they grow on this little girl's dome?"

"Say, lookit!" said Mayzie.

"It's wilting!" said Teacher. "How wonderful, Mayzie!
It soon will be dead! You'll be rid of that daisy!"
"In just a few minutes, our troubles will pass,"
Declared Dr. Grumm. "Take her back to the class."

DROOP!

Then the Principal saw a most terrible sight.
The daisy was dying. (And THAT was all right.)

But that daisy was part of poor Mayzie McGrew,
And Mayzie was starting to wilt away, too!

"Teacher," said Grumm, "you know what I think . . . !
They're *both* going to die! Hurry! Bring them a drink!
This is a problem," said Grumm with a frown.
"You take Mayzie away and you make her lie down!
You lock her up tight in that room down the hall.
There are quite a few numbers that I've got to call!"

"Get Mayzie's mother
    on the end of the line.
I need her here quickly
    while there is still time!"

Mayzie's mom asked,
    "What's all the fuss?
Goodness to Betsy!
    I'll be on the next bus!"

A call to the shoe store reached Mr. McGrew.

He answered while holding a customer's shoe.

"She is growing a WHAT? I'm coming right there!"

And he ran out of the shoe store with no time to spare.

"A doctor should see her," the Principal said,
"And an expert on plants like the one on her head."
So he called Dr. Eisenbart, who said, "Goodness gracious!
A child with a head that is partly herbaceous?
I simply must see this. I'll come over to you."
And his patient, though shirtless, came to see it, too.

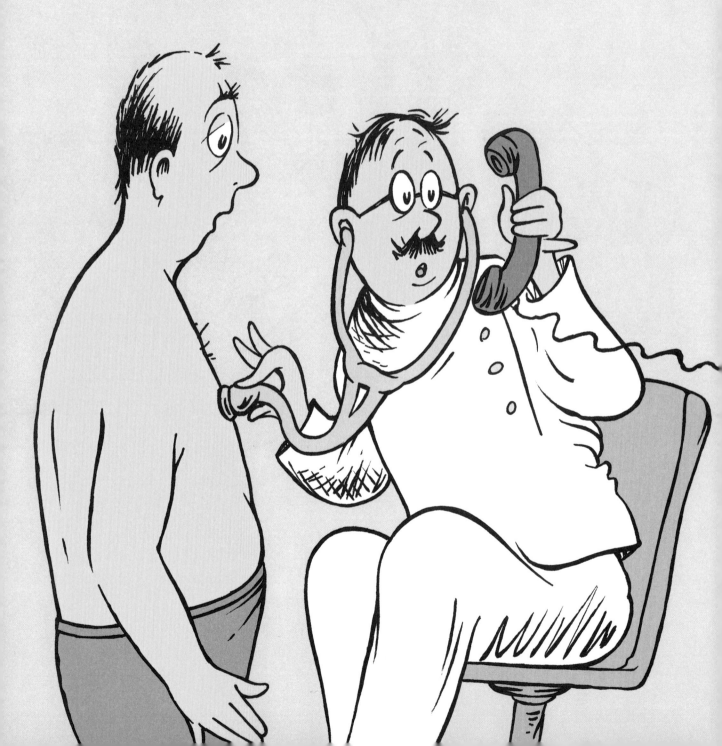

Then Grumm called Finch the Florist, who grabbed for his shears.
"I'll be there as fast as my truck can shift gears!"

Meanwhile, poor Mayzie lay down on a couch.
The daisy slumped down on its stem in a slouch.
But the window was open, because it was warm,
And the sweet-smelling daisy attracted a swarm . . .

OF BEES!

    Bees!

        Bees!

            Bees!

Mayzie jumped out the window. What else could she do?
But the faster she ran, the faster they flew.

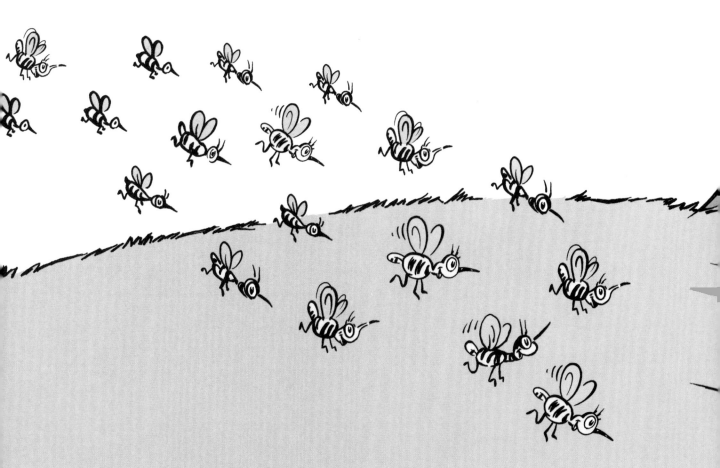

In the park she ran into Officer Thatcher.
(The bees on her heels were just starting to catch her.)
He said, "Wait a minute, kid. I'll be right back!"
And left Mayzie alone to fend off the attack!

But Thatcher returned with a fishbowl and bucket—
Into which went the fish from the bowl—then he stuck it . . .

On top of her head. She felt like a fool.

"Kid, I am taking you back to your school."

Principal Grumm didn't know what to do.

"It's worse!" cried Miss Sneetcher. "Much worse than we feared.

The daisy and Mayzie have both disappeared!"

Behind her came charging Mr. McGrew
(Chased by a customer chasing his shoe),
Finch the Florist, Dr. Eisenbart, too,
Dr. Eisenbart's patient, and Mrs. McGrew.

Then the door opened, and in came poor Mayzie,
Wearing the fishbowl protecting her daisy.

Then Officer Thatcher, who looked all around,
Said, "Anyone here know this kid that I found?"

"Mama!" cried Mayzie as she ran to her mother.
But Mrs. McGrew stepped back with a shudder.
"I think I feel faint," she just managed to utter.
"Stand back!" yelled the doctor as he looked about.
"Allow me some room to examine her sprout!"
The doctor approached, stethoscope to his ear . . .
But the wail of a siren was soon all he could hear!

"HIS HONOR, THE MAYOR!"

And then, without warning, the door opened wide . . .
And who but THE MAYOR should step right inside!
At Acting Important, there was none to compare.
He was best at long speeches, chock-full of hot air!

"I promise, my friends, that if I'm re-elected,
This daisy on Mayzie will be disconnected.
The law of our fathers is simple and sound:
Daisies belong and should stay in the ground.
The rest are illegal. We'll bar them from town!"

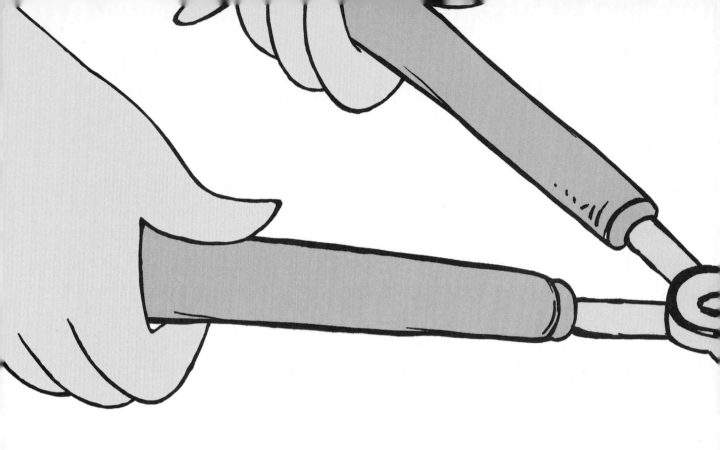

Then just as the Mayor finished his talk,
Finch the Florist began to quietly walk
And, standing directly right behind Mayzie,
Said, "I know the way to get rid of a daisy.
So there's a flower between her two ears?
I'll snip it clean off with my sharp pruning shears."
But Mayzie, she saw him and let out a screech.
She pushed him aside and raced out of his reach.

Mayzie ran from the school, headed straight out of town.
She came to a meadow and fell to the ground.
With her head in her hands, she lay all alone.
Her heart, it was broken. She could *never* go home.

"Nobody loves me!
Nobody loves me!
Nobody loves me!" she cried.

Nobody loved her . . . ? Poor Mayzie McGrew!
It's hard to believe such a thing could be true.
And maybe that's why, then, this daisy above,
When Mayzie, below, began talking of love . . .
Well, *you* know about daisies.
When love is in doubt,
The job of a daisy is, Try-and-Find-Out!

They love her . . .

They love her NOT!

They love her . . .

They love her NOT!

"Don't worry, Mayzie," said her daisy
As its last petal fell.
"They love you."
Then the stalk disappeared.

Well . . .

That's how it all happened. The thing went away.

And Mayzie McGrew is quite happy today . . .

Back at her studies, and doing just great
In all of her subjects in Room Number 8.

And concerning that daisy . . . you know that it *never*
Grew out of the top of her head again *ever*!
Errr . . . well, it *practically* never popped up there again.
Excepting, occasionally. Just now and then.

TING !

"And, after all . . . *I'm* getting used to it."

Daisy-Head Mayzie

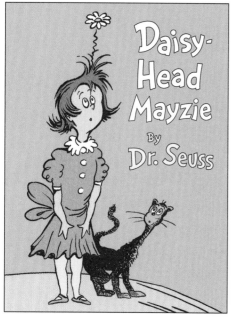

(Top) The 1995 edition.
(Bottom) The 2016 edition.

This edition of *Daisy-Head Mayzie* by Dr. Seuss is unlike any other you may have seen.

An earlier edition of *Daisy-Head Mayzie* was published by Random House in 1995 and remained in print until early 2016. If you compare the illustrations in the two books, you'll see a big difference. If you compare the words in the two books, you'll also see a difference. (Not as big, but a difference, nevertheless.)

How can this be?

To explain, let's look at *Mayzie's* roots. They go back, we believe, to the 1950s, when Ted Geisel—aka Dr. Seuss—wrote an animated film script called *Daisy-Head Mayzie.* Along with the script, Ted drew sketches for the main scenes in the film and one finished ink drawing of Mayzie.

Creating a script for an animated project was not new for Ted. He worked on many animated films during his career. While serving in the army during World War II, he was part of legendary film director Frank Capra's Signal Corps unit, producing animated training films for the armed forces.

After the war, Ted returned to writing children's books and also continued writing films. In 1950, he wrote the script for the Academy Award–winning animated film *Gerald McBoing-Boing.* In 1966, he wrote the script for the wildly successful animated television adaptation of his book *How the Grinch Stole Christmas!* And between 1969 and 1989, he would go on to write the scripts for another *nine* animated television specials.

We'll never know why Ted stopped work on *Daisy-Head Mayzie* and put the script in a drawer in his studio. Maybe he hoped to pick it up again at a later date. He often did that with stories and sketches. And clearly the character stayed on his mind, as a female character who sprouted a daisy from her head appeared in the 1976 book *The Cat's Quizzer.* Regardless, *Mayzie* would lie dormant for many years.

After a long illness, Ted Geisel died on September 24, 1991. Some time later, while cleaning his studio, Ted's wife Audrey found *Mayzie.* Since it was written prior to her marriage to Ted, it's quite possible that she'd never seen it before. Herb Cheyette—Ted's longtime agent—took the script and sketches to Hanna-Barbera Productions (producers of such beloved television shows as *The Flintstones, The Jetsons,* and *Scooby-Doo*), and a deal was made to bring *Mayzie* to life. On February 5, 1995, the animated special *Daisy-Head Mayzie* aired on television in the United States. It was a hit! The show was nominated for a primetime Emmy for Outstanding Animated Program. A picture book featuring illustrations based on the animation was published by Random House. Almost a quarter of a million copies were sold in its first year!

But as everyone who has read a book and then seen its film adaptation knows, a lot of changes happen when you take a written work and put it on-screen. Think of all the differences between the book and the animated television version of *How the Grinch Stole Christmas!* The plot was expanded so that the story would fill a half-hour television time slot. Songs were added, and the Grinch changed from black and white to green! Of course, these changes were made while Ted was alive, and he was very much involved in making them. (He not only wrote the screenplay and the song lyrics for *Grinch,* but was

A page from the 1976 book *The Cat's Quizzer.*

also a coproducer.) Filmmakers make these kind of changes for different reasons. Besides practical ones (like the need to expand the plot of a very short work), sometimes they want to emphasize a theme or a character's traits. Other times they try to solve things that they find problematic in an original work.

The most obvious change made when turning Ted's original script for *Mayzie* into a film was to the art. The sketches Ted drew for his script were redrawn in a new style. They now had a very different look.

In Ted's sketches, the people are normal-looking. The thing that disrupts the normalness is a small daisy—a symbol of innocence that usually (say, growing in a field and not from a child's head) couldn't be *less* threatening.

In the film adaptation, the characters are much more unusual-looking, and some of their hairstyles are positively surreal! In fact, even with a daisy sprouting from her head, Mayzie is not the most striking character in the television cartoon.

(Left) An illustration from the 1995 edition of *Daisy-Head Mayzie* based on the film animation. (Right) An illustration of the same scene from the 2016 edition based on Ted's original sketches.

Hanna-Barbera also added new characters and plot twists to Ted's script, including the Cat in the Hat as narrator of the story and a slick talent agent who convinces Daisy to leave school and seek her fortune as a celebrity—a decision she quickly regrets and makes right. Would Ted have made these changes? There's no way to be sure. What we *do* know is that he revised his own work, and that he was experienced at working with a team to produce animated films. He was aware that the process involved more than one person's vision.

Cathy Goldsmith was Ted Geisel's art director for the last eleven years of his life and served as art director for the 1995 book *Daisy-Head Mayzie.* Cathy was thrilled by the discovery of Ted's screenplay—and with the public's response to the 1995 edition of the book. But the publication of *another*

Mayzie's mother looks on as the talent agent (from the 1995 film and book) unrolls a contract for Mayzie to sign.

book twenty years later—Dr. Seuss's *What Pet Should I Get?*—got her thinking about *Mayzie* again.

"The response to *Pet* was so overwhelmingly positive, it made me realize what a hidden treasure we had in Ted's original work for *Daisy-Head Mayzie.* I'd always loved his sketches for *Mayzie.* They were simple and clear, and the clarity of his layouts kept the focus on Mayzie. There was nothing odd about Mayzie's world except for her daisy. The normalcy added irony and humor to Ted's story. I've always been hesitant to touch any of his original work. And admittedly, the *Mayzie* sketches needed to be cleaned up and finished. The script needed editing to function as a written story. But *Pet* gave us the confidence to do that. As we did with that book, we kept our changes to an absolute minimum, and did our best with the riches that Ted left us."

As was often the case, Ted had done his sketches for *Daisy-Head Mayzie* in pencil. In most of Ted's books, his final line work was done in ink. So the sketches needed to be rendered with an ink line to mirror the bulk of his work. This new edition of *Mayzie* uses Ted's original sketches as the basis for finished artwork, just as his original script was used as the basis for the text. Ted's one piece of finished line art was used for the cover.

Below is an example of one of Ted's pencil sketches and the resulting finished line art:

(Left)
Pencil sketch.
(Right)
Finished ink
line art.

Once the line art was completed, color needed to be added. There are only three titles where Ted painted full-color art for a book: *Happy Birthday to You!, McElligot's Pool,* and *I Can Lick Thirty Tigers Today! And Other Stories.* For his other books, color was added to the ink line art based on color specifications that Ted provided.

A spread from *Did I Ever Tell You How Lucky You Are?,* colored by Ted and marked with numbers to show color specifications.

For this edition of *Mayzie,* Cathy Goldsmith worked out the color specs. "I started by thinking about Mayzie—what color should her hair be? What color should her dress be? The other characters and locations had to be colored so the focus remained on Mayzie and her daisy. To do this, I started by using colored pencils on copies of the line art, just as Ted did when he worked on books. This helped me to see if the colors I had in mind worked well when placed together on a page. Once I had the basic colors worked out, I moved to the computer, which is *not* something that Ted did. The computer helps me to zero in on exactly what shade of blue is needed, what shade of yellow, etc."

It was also challenging to make *Mayzie* work as a book while remaining as true to Ted's original as possible. Animation can show action on-screen without any words. In a book, images don't move, so you need words to show action. In some places, Ted's script indicated action to take place without any words. To turn his script into a book, the editors at Random House needed to write words—transitions and a few rhymed stanzas—that moved the story along.

Something you will find in *every* version of *Daisy-Head Mayzie* (Ted's screenplay, the Hanna-Barbera television special, and both editions of the book) is a central female character. This is special because Mayzie is one of the few female protagonists to be found in any Seuss book. A 1990 essay by novelist Alison Lurie in *The New York Review of Books* pointed out this lack of female characters. Ted's response to the criticism was that most of his characters were animals, "and if [Lurie] can identify their sex, I'll remember her in my will." Nevertheless, besides Miss Bonkers from *Hooray for Diffendoofer Day!* and the female narrator of the second half of *The Shape of Me and Other Stuff,* there are few *clearly* female Seussian main characters.

Daisy-Head Mayzie is a story about celebrating those qualities that make each of us unique. It's a theme Ted addressed many times in his work, most especially in *Happy Birthday to You!* This particular edition of *Daisy-Head Mayzie* comes as close as we can to Ted Geisel's unique vision. We hope that it grows on you (although not from the top of your head), and that it inspires you to celebrate those special qualities that make you *you.*